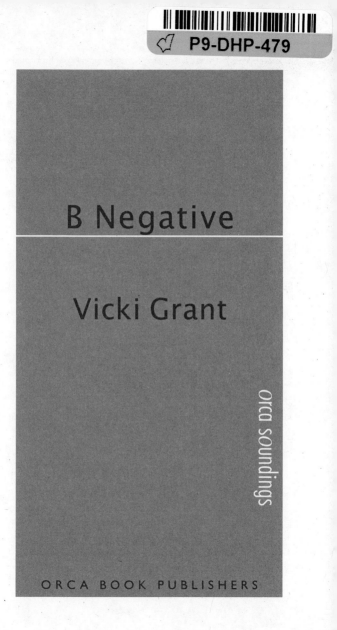

B Negative

Vicki Grant

orca soundings

ORCA BOOK PUBLISHERS

Library and Archives Canada Cataloguing in Publication

Grant, Vicki
B negative / Vicki Grant.
(Orca soundings)

Issued also in electronic formats.
ISBN 978-1-55469-842-4 (bound).--ISBN 978-1-55469-841-7 (pbk.)

I. Title. II. Series: Orca soundings
PS8613.R367B12 2011   JC813'.6   C2010-908062-9

First published in the United States, 2011
Library of Congress Control Number: 2010942086

Summary: When Paddy discovers that the man he thought was his father isn't, he struggles to put his life back together.

MIX
Paper from
responsible sources
FSC™ C016245

Orca Book Publishers is dedicated to preserving the environment and has printed this book on paper certified by the Forest Stewardship Council.

Orca Book Publishers gratefully acknowledges the support for its publishing programs provided by the following agencies: the Government of Canada through the Canada Book Fund and the Canada Council for the Arts, and the Province of British Columbia through the BC Arts Council and the Book Publishing Tax Credit.

Cover design by Teresa Bubela
Cover photography by Getty Images

ORCA BOOK PUBLISHERS
PO Box 5626, Stn. B
Victoria, BC Canada
V8R 6S4

ORCA BOOK PUBLISHERS
PO Box 468
Custer, WA USA
98240-0468

www.orcabook.com
Printed and bound in Canada.

14 13 12 11 • 4 3 2 1

To Linda Alexander,
for always being positive.

Chapter One

Everything's fine.

There's a big slab of barbecued steak in front of me. The sun is shining. My girlfriend's here. The little kids are happy.

So why am I so pissed off then?

I don't know.

No. I do know. It's Anthony. (Like that's a surprise. When is it *not* Anthony?)

Can't he shut up?

Does he honestly believe I'm interested in his advice?

Mom married him—what? Thirteen years ago? That means he's known me since I was five. You'd think he'd have a clue by now.

But no. Having a clue would require him to actually listen to someone other than himself, and that ain't gonna happen anytime soon.

"If I were you," he's saying, "I'd forget about doing something practical for the moment. I'd pursue my music. I see real promise in you." He turns down his chin and looks me right in the eye.

Another person might mistake that for sincerity, but I'm not that easy to fool. I know what he's doing. He's checking his reflection in my pupils. The guy's so full of himself I'm surprised he has room for the steak.

And that reminds me. Isn't he supposed to be a vegan? I distinctly remember him ruining another family dinner over his new diet. He kept nagging us about all the toxins we were shoveling into our mouths. Meanwhile, he was "honoring" *his* body with raw bean sprouts.

He has a hunk of meat on the end of his fork and is pointing it at me. Blood is dripping onto the table.

"I could have gone into law. That's what my parents wanted me to do, of course. Follow the family tradition. But that just wasn't my thing. Instead I decided to follow"—big pause here—"my heart. I chose the theater. I've never regretted it."

He tosses back his hair. He loves his hair. Tara says there's no way those blond streaks up front are natural. That used to embarrass me. Now it just makes me laugh. I love picturing him in the black cape with the little pieces of tinfoil all over his head, looking like the total conceited jackass that he is.

Anthony takes a bite and puts his hand on my shoulder. "Follow your heart," he says again, only this time he's chewing right in my ear.

Nice.

My mother looks up from her salad and her eyes go watery. This touching little moment has obviously moved her.

I don't get it. She's a smart woman. How can she still believe his crap?

I keep eating away as if there's no problem, but the truth is I'm danger-ously close to exploding. Would he just get his frigging hand off me? I'm one second away from telling him to shut his face. I wouldn't mind blowing a few giant holes in his story while I'm at it too.

For instance: He chose "the theater"? Please.

Playing "satisfied homeowner" in a thirty-second TV commercial for a miracle toilet plunger is not the theater.

You don't have to be Brad Pitt to say, "Yours for just three payments of $19.95!"

And as for not regretting his decision—why would he? Life's good for Anthony Paul Wishart. He sits around the house all day doing nothing.

No, I'm sorry. That's wrong. He doesn't do nothing. He does yoga. He does some serious time in front of the television. And, of course, he does his hair. That's very important. He has to look his best for his "career."

Just thinking that makes me want to kill him. How can a grown man with two little kids, a wife and a stepson live like that?

Why do I even ask? I know the answer.

Chapter Two

My father. That's the answer.

Like, I mean, John Armstrong. My real father. He works hard because he actually feels responsible for someone other than himself. He lives in some crappy little apartment and never goes out or buys himself anything new. All his money goes to child support payments.

Which just happen to be enough to cover the mortgage on the house Anthony hangs around in all day. How convenient.

Mom pays the other expenses by working as a receptionist at Child Welfare International. It's a nonprofit organization so they don't pay much, but it's something. (So much for *her* acting career. She, at least, had enough pride to go out and get a real job when the bills started piling up.)

I only get a couple of shifts a week at the hardware store, but I pitch in what I can too.

I look across the table at Tara. I thought I was doing a pretty good job of faking nice, but I clearly haven't fooled her. I guess after three years with me she knows what's going through my head. She dips a French fry in ketchup and puts it in her mouth. She's looking at me the whole time. Her eyes are telling me to calm down.

Anthony drops his hand onto his thigh with a big slap. He leans back in his chair and stretches his legs out in front of him. It's only June and they're already seriously tanned.

"So, Paddy, what'll it be? There are lots of great music colleges who'd be lucky to have you, you know. Or perhaps you'd rather just take the band on the road. Given any thought to that? The year I spent touring *Grease* with the Colchester County Musical Theater Society was perhaps the most interesting—and exciting—period of my…"

I can't listen to this again. He's crazy. He wants me to go to music college now? Who's going to pay for that? Not Anthony, that's for sure. He's just assuming Dad will foot the bill.

As for his other suggestion— please. Go on the road? Like our lame band would make any money that way. Anthony might have trouble understanding this, but being able to support myself actually matters to me.

I'd love to bring that up right now but I can't. It would get too ugly. I stop chewing and clamp down on the meat in my mouth. It's like biting a bullet to take your mind off the pain. The smear of ketchup on my plate makes me think of blood. I stare at it and try to blank Anthony out.

Tara drops her fork. The noise makes me look up. It wasn't an accident. She says, "Sorry. Clumsy me!" but she's got that look in her eyes again. I don't know if I see her shake her head or I just sense it. She picks up her fork and makes a big point of sawing off a piece of meat. *Steak*, she's reminding me. *Your mother paid a lot of money for it. Ignore Anthony. Don't ruin this for her.*

Fine. I start chewing really loud like I'm some cartoon slob. Tara's eyes go all shiny and she has to bite her lip to stop from smiling. I put a big grin on my face and say, "Mmmm. You're some cook, Mom. This is delicious."

"Aw, thanks, honey," she says. I can see how happy that makes her. Never hurts to keep the ladies happy.

I look around the table.

Olivia is drawing something on her plate in ketchup. She loves to draw.

Marlon is standing beside Mom with his hands on her face, begging to stay up to watch Power Ponies tonight. Mom's shushing him but she's laughing too. She knows she's going to give in.

Everyone's enjoying themselves. Life is good—even if Anthony has started yammering on again about my "brilliant future."

Tara's right. The guy's a douche bag, but pointing that out would only upset the non-douche-bag members of my family.

I wink at her. She stabs at her salad and puts a giant piece of lettuce in her mouth. She gets bright orange dressing all over her chin. "Aw. Gross," I say. People forget about Anthony for a second and look at Tara. Everyone laughs.

You'd think Anthony would take this opportunity to shut up—but no such luck.

"Seriously, Paddy," he says. "High school's behind you. You can do anything you want with your life now. So what'll it be? Music college or the tour?"

I try to concentrate on dinner, but my brain is suddenly just, like, flooded with rage.

Those are my choices? Says who?

Anthony?

How does he know what I want to do? What does it even matter to him? He's not my father.

Tara's face has gone flat and white. She mouths the word, "Don't." She can feel the pressure ramping up again even if Anthony can't.

I take a breath. Olivia is braiding Tara's hair now. Marlon's on Mom's lap. Dinner's almost over. *Just hold on.*

All I have to do is answer. Say something. *Anything.* It doesn't matter. It's not like Anthony actually cares what I think.

I almost get my mouth open, but then I make the mistake of looking at him. He's leaning back with his hands behind his head. He's got this "rugged guy" smile on his face, like the one he used in that so-called modeling job for the Dugger's Menswear flyer. He has one too many buttons undone on his shirt.

He better not be doing that for Tara's benefit.

He sticks his foot out and jabs me in the leg. "C'mon, Paddy. What? What's it going to be?"

He's either totally stunned or he's taunting me.

I can't stand the guy. I can't even stand the thought of him *thinking* I can stand him.

I wipe my mouth with the back of my hand. I sort of smile. Tara gives me that little headshake again.

"Neither, actually," I say to him. "I'm joining the Army."

Chapter Three

Anthony thinks I'm joking. He throws back his head and laughs. (Even his laugh is bullshit.)

The truth is I didn't really mean it. I just wanted to say something that would irritate him but still sound like an answer. Joining the Army just sort of popped into my head. I knew he'd hate it.

He likes to think of himself as a pacifist. Actually, he's just too lazy to fight for anything.

But now that I've said it, I realize it's not a bad idea. It'd be a regular paycheck. And it would make Dad happy. He likes the military. He was in the Navy for twenty years until he retired and took a job as a commissionaire.

I can always play in a band in my spare time.

"I'm not kidding," I say. "I'm signing up next week." I use my baby finger to pick some food out from between my molars. That's how much Anthony's opinion means to me.

His chair slams back onto the floor.

"The Army!" He makes it sound like I'm joining the circus—though knowing Anthony, he'd probably think that was perfectly fine. (Just what we need. Another freak in the family.)

I shrug. "Yeah, the Army."

He stretches out the fingers on his right hand and turns to Mom. "Maura!" he says. He's too lazy to even fight his *own* battles.

I'm loving this. He's so helpless— he's so *hope*less. Anthony's big problem is that he thinks he's so frigging gorgeous he should rule the world. He's obviously watched too many Disney cartoons. That's the only place they make you prince just because you're pretty.

I make sure there's no smile showing on my face and then I turn and look at Mom too.

She's fussing with her collar and her eyes have gone all teary again.

Damn.

I didn't mean to upset her.

Marlon says, "Paddy's joining the Army? Yay!"

Mom says, "Quiet, Marlon, please," but he jumps off her knee and starts racing around the table pretending to shoot everyone.

"Bang! Bang! Bang! You're dead!"

Anthony looks at me. "Is that what you want to do? Kill people? Huh? Or maybe you'd prefer to *get* killed?"

Olivia stops braiding Tara's hair. She looks at me. Her bottom lip starts to quiver. Then she bursts into tears. "I don't want Paddy to die!"

Anthony puts on this fake smile. "Good work," he says to me. "Look what you did to your little sister…" Olivia runs into his arms, sobbing.

I turn to look at Tara. I'm sort of hoping she'll be laughing at this. I mean, it's so ridiculous. What else can you do?

Tara's got three scraggly braids on the side of her head. Her arms are crossed so tight that her collarbones are all sticking out and webbed with skin. They make me think of a bat's wing. She's not laughing.

She's mad at me too.

Chapter Four

We're in the car outside Tara's apartment building. It's dark now. She's staring straight out the windshield, playing with her gum. She pulls it out in a long string, then chews it back in. She's doing that so she doesn't have to talk to me.

"What?" I say.

She looks at me then turns back and looks out the windshield again.

"C'mon. What?" I say. I'm trying not to laugh.

We do this sometimes. We get in these little fights and we both say we hate it, but the truth is, it's kind of fun.

Tara's one of those skinny girls who doesn't smile much. I remember when I first met her, I used to think she was always pissed off about something. I didn't like her very much. Then I got to know her and realized she's not mad. It's just the way she holds her face. She's actually prettier when she smiles.

I know she's dying to tell me what a jerk I am for upsetting everyone. I can handle that. Eventually I'll come up with something that will make her laugh, and we'll be okay again.

No use wasting time. The sooner we get things started, the sooner we can get this over with and move on to the good stuff.

"C'mon," I say again and give her a little poke in the ribs.

She slaps my hand away.

"Asshole," she says.

It's not the first time she's called me that, but her tone is different now. It takes me a second to process it.

"Seriously?" I say. "You're actually mad?"

She turns her head toward me really slowly. She squints up her eyes, then drops her jaw. I take that as a yes.

"What?" I say. "What's the problem?"

"You're an idiot."

"Anthony's the idiot."

"Oh, yeah? Really? He's not the one joining the Army."

So that's what she's pissed about.

I sort of laugh. "Look," I start, but then I don't know what to say. If I admit I said I'm signing up just to bug Anthony,

I really will look like an asshole. Worse, she'll make me un-say it. She'll make me back down and not go. There's no way I can do that now. Not after the fight Anthony and I had. He went totally insane. I don't want to give him a reason to think he had any right to.

She leans her back against the car door and glares at me. She's a master of the silent treatment. I clear my throat. "It's just the Army. Lots of people join the Army."

She coughs like that's a stupid thing to say. It's so typical Tara.

Now we're both mad.

I try to keep my temper under control. "It's a real job," I say. "Real money. I could learn a skill too. The Army pays for your education, you know."

Truth is, I'm not a hundred-percent sure about that, but it worked. It softens her up a bit. Tara understands money. Or at least what it's like not to have any.

If I ever feel sorry for myself, I just have to look at how she and her mother live. At least I have a father helping out.

She brushes her hair off her face. That's a good sign. She still wants to look nice for me. I go in to close the deal. "And I think I'd really like it too."

She spits out her gum and squeezes it into a little scrap of paper. "Oh, please. Cut the crap, Paddy. What kind of moron do you think I am? You wouldn't like the Army. You like getting up at six AM? You like following orders? You like shooting people?"

"Not everyone in the Army shoots people."

"Fine. That's not the point."

"What is the point then?"

I suddenly realize she's going to cry, and that really freaks me out. Tara never cries. She roots around in her pocket for another piece of gum. She tries to push it through the bubble wrap but can't and biffs the whole package on the floor.

She looks right at me. Her mouth has gone tiny, but at least she's managing to hold back the tears.

"The point is, Paddy…" She takes a big loud breath in through her nose. "The point is, that you could have talked to me first. Look. I don't want to marry you. A year from now I might not even want to go out with you. But I am your frigging girlfriend now. I would like to talk to you about these things, you know.

"And maybe if I'd had the chance to talk to you, we could have avoided that little scene tonight. I could have convinced you that you're not really a soldier type of guy. Maybe—believe it or not—Anthony's right. You really would be a whole lot happier playing your guitar at some cheesy bar, rather than out marching around some-where in your little GI Joe costume."

I want to defend myself. Before I can think of something to say, though, she throws her hand up in the air and is at me again.

"Or maybe I wouldn't have been able to talk you out of it, and you know what? That would have been kind of okay, too, because at least—at least!—you would have shown that you cared a little bit about me and my opinion. Instead, you make me feel like I'm just some casual acquaintance. Some Facebook friend. Someone you just hang out with for a while and then dump when you find something better to do with your time."

"Tara," I say, "that's not true. You know that. I—" But she's got her arms out straight in front of her like I'm going to attack her or something. She's shaking her head at me.

"Too late for that, Paddy."

"Tara…" I lean over and put my hand on her thigh. I look her in the eyes. I smile at her.

"Trying to charm me, are you?" Her lip curls up. "It's not working—and you know what's even worse? You'll like this…" She laughs. "That's exactly what Anthony would do under the circumstances."

I take my hand off her leg and lean back into my seat. I can feel my blood pounding. Tara's always known how to go for the jugular.

But that's fine. I've got 726 other Facebook friends. I don't need her.

She waits for me to say something back, but I don't.

I can't believe I used to think she was pretty.

She slams the door and I floor it.

Chapter Five

Mom's not the type to get mad or tell you what to do, but I can see she's not happy about me going into the Army. I almost wish she'd just say so. In fact, I almost wish she'd start crying or screaming about it. That, at least, would give me an option. I could back down without looking like I'm giving in to Anthony—or to Tara. I'd be doing it for Mom.

But she doesn't even mention it. She looks a bit sad, I guess, but Mom always looks a bit sad even when she's smiling. She did ask where Tara's been the last few days, but when I went, "Ah, we're like, you know...," she just kind of grimaced and said, "Oh." She didn't bring it up again.

The only thing Mom actually said was that she'd like me to get a complete medical before I sign up. I told her the Army would do that, but she said, "Please...," and turned away really quickly. So I said, "Sure."

I don't know why it means so much to her, but I have an idea. Dr. Wallace is the guy who delivered me. I've been seeing him all my life. Mom must figure he could talk some sense into me.

She got him to tell me about birth control and STDs when I reached puberty, so it's not as if she hasn't tried it before.

We drive downtown together. Mom's office is just around the corner from the doctor's, so it's easy for both of us. We stop at the Fair Trade Coffee Shop and she insists we each get a latte. That makes me nervous. Seven bucks is too much for her to be spending on coffee—but I go along with it anyway. It makes Mom happy, and I could use the caffeine. (I haven't been sleeping so well since that thing with Tara.)

We're at the counter waiting for our order. Mom is telling me—again—to ask Dr. Wallace to check out the rash on my elbow. A lady taps her on the shoulder and says, "Maura?"

It's like someone turned on a switch. Mom's face lights up and she suddenly looks like she did in old pictures of herself. She squeals, "Nadine!" They hug, hold each other out at arm's length, then hug again.

Mom smiles and shakes her head and says, "You look fabulous! What are you doing back in town?"

"Business. Just a quick trip. I didn't know you still lived here! You look fabulous too. How long has it been? I'm scared to ask."

"Oh, gee…" Mom puts her hand on her chin. "Must be eighteen, no, more like nineteen years. It *was* nineteen years, because we did the play in February, right?"

She suddenly remembers me. "Oh, honey, sorry. This is my friend, Nadine Sommers. Nadine and I met when we put on *Anne of Green Gables* at the Orpheus. I just had a small role, but Nadine and Anthony both had lead roles."

"Anthony? Anthony Wishart?" Nadine obviously hasn't heard that name in a while. "Do you ever see him anymore?"

That makes me laugh.

"We're married," Mom says and blushes.

Now Nadine laughs too. "Oh, congratulations!" She looks at me. "This must be your son."

"Oh, sorry, yes. Paddy."

Nadine shakes my hand. "Wow. The resemblance is amazing. I guess you hear that all the time. So what do you do? Still in school?"

"I just graduated and now I'm…"

The barrista calls out our order and Mom swings around like it's some big emergency. She's holding her purse and her umbrella and trying to take the lattes too. She knocks the edge of the counter and a little coffee splashes on Nadine's shoe.

Nadine dabs it off with a napkin. It's nothing major, but Mom's suddenly all flustered.

"Oh! Sorry! What's the matter with me? I guess I'm just nervous, seeing you and everything. And I'm late too. I have to run. Any chance we could get together for a bite sometime?"

They exchange email addresses and kiss and hug. Then Mom's pulling me out the door, and I'm halfway down the street before I can get her to stop.

"Geez, Mom, what's with you? Slow down, would you?"

She stops, lets go of me, then takes a few deep breaths. It's like she's trying to pull herself together.

"Sorry," she says. "Sorry. You know me. I hate being late. I was worried you were going to miss your doctor's appointment and…"

I don't believe her. She's always late. That's not what's bugging her.

"Relax. It's okay." I smile. "Want me to drop by when I'm done? Maybe we can go out for lunch together or something."

Whatever's upsetting her will probably be over by then.

"Oh, honey, that sounds great—but I can't. I'm really busy today. In fact—oh, gee, look at the time. I better go."

She gives me a peck on the cheek and hurries off down the street.

She waves at me when she gets to the corner. I realize I haven't moved. I'm staring at her like a little kid, scared to see his mommy leave.

I turn and start walking to the doctor's. I laugh at myself.

What's my problem? Why am I making such a big deal of this? She's just busy. There's that big Parent-Child Conference next month. She's probably worried about it. She's always been a bit high-strung.

That almost makes me feel better—
but something about the way she looked
at me still doesn't sit quite right.

I'm walking in Dr. Wallace's door
when I realize what it is. I see Mom's
face again and I know she's not worried
about the conference.

Mom's embarrassed of me.

Chapter Six

Mom hustled us out of the coffee shop before I could tell Nadine I was joining the Army. Then she didn't want me dropping by the office.

That's what this is about. She's embarrassed to have a soldier for a son. She doesn't want anyone to know.

I remember Dad saying how Mom's hippie friends all talk about letting people be whoever they want to be—but they aren't so good at following through on it. I understand what he meant now.

My instincts were right about another thing too.

I'm putting my shirt back on after my checkup and getting ready to go when Dr. Wallace says, "So—I understand you're enlisting."

Just like I thought. Mom *did* ask him to have a little chat with me.

I say, "Yeah, it's a good way to get my education." He agrees—or at least *sounds* like he agrees. But then he goes on and on about my musical abilities and the reality of actually going to war and the stress that would put on my family.

I nod like I've thought about all that. I say, "I appreciate your concern but I've pretty much made up my mind."

I do up the last two buttons. He goes to say something else, but I smile in the

35

cockiest way I can and he stops. He clicks his teeth and says, "Well, good then."

We both know I'm old enough to make my own decisions.

He taps his pen on the desk. There's this kind of awkward pause. I don't want him to feel bad. I like the guy. I say, "So am I healthy? Good to go?"

He says, "Oh, yeah. You're the picture of health."

He looks at my chart. "Let's see... a hundred and eighty-two pounds— good. Blood pressure—good. Heart-rate of an Olympic runner..."

He flips the page. "Haven't done your blood work in a while, but let's see what we had last time...Hmm."

He raises his eyebrows.

"What?" I say.

"Nothing. I just see your blood type is B negative."

"Is that bad?"

He waves his hand at me. "No. Not at all. It's somewhat rare so it's a little hard to come by if you need a transfusion—but, ah…"

His voice trails off as if he just said something wrong.

What's with everyone? Just because I'm joining the Army doesn't mean I'm going to get my legs blown off.

Dr. Wallace closes the file and pushes it to the side of his desk.

"Nothing to worry about," he says, all cheery again. He stands up and shakes my hand. "Take care of yourself now, Paddy." He sounds like he really means it.

Chapter Seven

It's not any easier telling the guys in the band that I'm leaving either. We've been together since junior high. We still aren't great musicians but we can usually get the crowd on their feet. In fact, we're a bit of local success story. These days we never have any problem filling the legion hall, and we actually got a decent number of hits on our last YouTube video, even with the sound and lighting problems. Just the same, it's not like any of us really thinks we're going to make a living doing this. Most gigs bring in just enough to cover equipment rental and, let's say, *refreshments*.

So I figure it's going to be kind of sad leaving the band, but no one's really going to care that much.

Wrong.

We're sitting in Jasper's basement. It's always been kind of a happy place for me. This is where I've written some of our best songs. But now everybody is either glaring at me or stretched out on one of the moldy couches, pretending I'm not here.

Riley says he's already booked a couple of gigs for the fall. He doesn't think there will be time to find someone to replace me.

I promise to stay as long as I can, but it pisses me off. Why does everybody act like this is about their life, not mine?

I get up to leave. A couple of the guys grunt. That's as close as they get to saying goodbye.

I'm walking home, kicking stones out of my way and cursing to myself. I'm mad at Riley and the guys, but I'm thinking about Tara. Riley talking about "replacing" me is what did it.

Gavin McKnight has been after Tara as long as I've known him. I never liked the way Will Chan looked at her either.

I realize that the band might have trouble replacing me, but Tara won't.

I suddenly want to call her. I want to talk to her. I want to make her laugh. Make her see things my way.

Then I remember what she said about Anthony—and what a jerk she can be—so I don't.

I call someone I can count on instead.

I call Dad.

Chapter Eight

We arrange to meet the next day at his favorite restaurant. The Bluenose isn't fancy but the food's good, and it's not far from Dad's work.

He's been out of the Navy since I was twelve, but you'd never know it to look at him. Dad still keeps his hair short and walks like he's in a parade. He's always telling me to stand up straight, because it makes you look taller. He might need the extra inches—he's maybe five foot seven—but I don't. I tower over the guy.

He shakes my hand and we take a booth in the front with a good view of the street.

"I was wondering when you were going to get around to telling me," he says. He puts his wallet on the table beside his coffee cup. "Your mother mentioned you've made some plans."

I thought he'd look happier than he does.

"Yeah," I say.

"The Army," he says.

"Yeah." I laugh. I get it. "I guess you would have preferred the Navy."

He rolls his eyes. "No kidding. A landlubber. My old shipmates are going to wonder what type of job I did raising my kid."

Martha comes over and pours us two cups of coffee. She doesn't even bother with a menu. "Chowder, club sandwich, two rice puddings?"

I wouldn't mind trying something different for a change, but Dad says, "Of course."

She puts her finger to her lips. "I'm not talking to you, Johnnie. I'm talking to the good-looking one." She winks at me.

I say, "Of course!" as if there was never any doubt.

"Why does it sound so much better when he says it?" She kind of cradles her coffee pot in her arms and sighs. "For the life of me, I don't know how an old bulldog like you managed to produce something as gorgeous as this...Must have skipped a generation."

She elbows Dad, and he does that ha-ha laugh of his. Even though he's not the kind of guy to show his emotions— let alone *admit* that he actually has any—I can tell he's proud of me.

Not that I ever doubted it.

The guy is the world's most devoted dad. (He even has the coffee cup to prove it.) He was at sea a lot when I was a kid but he made up for it when he was home. He went to all my games, all the school plays, all the concerts. Taught me to catch a ball, change a tire, build a go-cart. Had me over every weekend even if it meant he had to sleep on the couch. He never even dated after Mom and he split up. It was all about me.

Now he calls me once a week. A couple of times a month we go to the Bluenose. A couple of times a year we go fishing. When I've got a gig, he goes to that.

Otherwise? He works. Goes to the gym. Goes home.

That's his life.

I'm surprised he even mentioned his old Navy buddies. He stopped drinking five years ago. I bet he hasn't seen them since.

He takes a sip of coffee. I can see it burns his lip. It always does. I used to wonder why he didn't just blow on it or wait until it cooled down a bit but I don't anymore. I realize that for Dad it's all part of manning up. You do what you have to do and keep quiet about it. Sometimes that means sacrificing your life for your kid's. Sometimes that means choking down burning hot coffee.

He pushes his mug out of the way. "So when do you start?"

"Don't know. Haven't really done anything about it yet except email the recruiter and get a medical."

"How'd you check out?"

I shrug. "Perfect physical specimen apparently. Other than my blood, I guess."

"Your blood?" Dad's so tough sometimes I forget what an old lady he can be.

"It's nothing," I say.

Martha comes by with a basket of rolls. He smiles at her, but he's got one hand gripping the side of the table like he's bracing for bad news.

"What do you mean nothing?" he says as soon as she's gone.

"Nothing to worry about. I'm B negative, that's all."

He settles back into his seat. "Didn't know that."

"Why should you?" I say. I take a sip of coffee. It's still hot but bearable.

He looks out the window. His face isn't giving much away, but I can tell he's upset about something.

"What?" I say. "Don't look so worried. There's nothing the matter with B-negative blood."

"No. It's not that." He leans back in his seat.

"What then?"

He surprises me. He actually answers.

"Just getting sentimental, I guess. Makes me realize how much of your childhood I missed, and now look at you. All grown up."

"Dad...," I say. "You're a great father. You—"

"What's up with the band these days?" he says, then takes another sip of coffee.

So much for our heart-to-heart talk. It almost makes me laugh.

I give him a cleaned-up version of my discussion with the guys. He doesn't need the gory details. I don't want him mad at them just because he thinks they treated me badly. He kind of lacks perspective when it comes to me.

The food arrives and Martha flirts with us until another customer waves her over. We talk about military life— the discipline, the opportunities, the travel, the pension. I'm starting to feel better about joining up. I turned eighteen in November, but this is the first time I've really felt like an adult. I'm making a decision. I'm being responsible. I'm acting like a man.

Dad gets it. He doesn't question my choice.

We finish our rice pudding. We probably should get going so Martha can clear our table, but we hang around talking for a while. I'm usually the one rushing to go, but that's because I usually have a girlfriend or a band practice to get to. Now I've got time to spare.

Dad pulls out a picture and starts talking about the old boat he just bought. The *Julie-Anne*. He only paid eight hundred bucks for it and it'll probably sink before he has a chance to sail it. But you wouldn't know that by the look on his face. He's like a little kid.

I push his shoulder. "You sailed destroyers for twenty years and now you're all excited about some leaky old fishing boat?"

He gives a wheezy laugh, and out of habit starts fumbling around for the cigarettes he hasn't smoked in five years. (Another thing he gave up for me.)

"Yup. Sad, ain't it? But the *Julie-Anne* is mine. That's the difference. No 'Yes, sir. No, sir' for me anymore. I'm the admiral of this fleet."

I get a little twinge at the "Yes, sir. No, sir" thing. I remember Tara saying how I didn't like taking orders. I tell myself to forget it. There are people you should worry about and people you shouldn't waste your time on. I ask Dad where he keeps the boat and what he plans to do with it.

He tells me it's tied up way out in Halibut Cove because he'll be damned if he'll pay the crazy mooring fees they have in the city.

He stops talking all of a sudden, and I think for a second he's got heartburn or something. Then he looks away. He clears his throat. He asks if I'd like to get out for a couple of nights on the boat with him before I leave.

I realize why he never married again. If it's this hard asking your own son on a boat ride, imagine how hard it would be asking a woman on a date.

I say, "Sure. Sounds great," but I don't hear his answer. For some reason, I'm thinking about Tara again. My body sort of flip-flops every time I think of her. I love her. I hate her. I love her again.

This is ridiculous. I gulp down the last of my coffee. I don't need her. There are lots of other girls.

Christie Fox, for instance. She's pretty. And she actually smiles occasionally.

I'm going to call her.

Martha brings the bill. Dad pays in cash and leaves too big a tip, as usual. She tries to give part of it back, but he won't take it.

That gets me thinking too.

She's a little younger than Dad but not much. Mom was *way* younger. Martha's not bad-looking either, and they seem to like each other.

Maybe I could convince him to ask her out.

Dad and I shake hands on the sidewalk and make plans to go on the boat ride next weekend.

Martha's at the cash ringing out another customer. Dad waves at her as he walks past.

I've never had any problems with girls. Maybe I could give him some pointers. Maybe I could help *him* for a change.

Chapter Nine

I get up early the next day. Our neighbors are moving and they need some help with the hide-a-bed. Anthony says his back is bothering him so he can't do it. A week ago that would have driven me crazy, but now—who cares? I'm going to be gone soon.

The husband and I manage to get the couch out, but there's still a pile of boxes to move so I help with those too.

I get home around eleven. I'm craving a raspberry slushie, but I pour myself a glass of water instead. Tara works next door to the convenience store. I don't need a slushie that bad.

I suck back two glasses of water and decide to call Christie. No point wasting any more time.

Christie's surprised about Tara and me, but after I explain the situation, she doesn't hesitate. We're going for dinner Thursday at the Nectar House. I'm going to have a good job soon. I can afford to take her someplace nice.

If Tara gets upset about that, too bad. She was the one who didn't think it was a good idea for me to get a real job. She was the one who left.

I pull off my sweaty clothes and get in the shower. I make a mental list of things I have to do before I leave.

That boat ride with Dad.

Some quality time with the little kids, especially Olivia. She's been hanging off me ever since that dinner.

I also want to have one last gig with the band. Riley texted me last night. Jasper's cousin's a decent guitar player and said he'd step in for me. The guys are apparently ready to forgive me after all.

I've got this idea for a song that I want to try out before I go. It's called "B Negative." It's still just a rough concept, but I think there's something there. The basic idea is that I've made this big life decision and everyone is, like, *be-ing negative* about it except me.

The funny thing is that I'm the one with the-B negative blood. Dr. Wallace said something about B negative being perfectly good, just unusual, and I thought I could maybe work that in too.

I hum this little riff that's been going through my head for a while. I try it again faster. It's starting to seem like a more upbeat song than I thought it was going to be.

I get out of the shower and towel myself dry. I feel good. Good about the Army. Good about the song. Good about Christie.

I wait until Anthony goes out for his run before I head downstairs. I check my email. Nothing from the recruiter yet, or Tara for that matter, but I wasn't expecting anything from her.

There is an email from Dad, though, saying he's going to have to cancel our boat ride.

It kind of catches me off guard.

I never got an email from Dad before. He always calls. He's not a big writer. Even all that time he was at sea, the most he ever sent home was a postcard.

And he's never canceled anything before either.

I write back, *You not talking to me now or something?* but then delete it. Dad might not know I'm joking. Instead I put *No problem. Still on for lunch at the Bluenose next week?* and send it.

I go into the kitchen to get something to eat. I notice the tap dripping. Typical Anthony. You can't even trust him to turn off the water when he's finished with it.

I turn the handle hard. The water keeps dripping.

I'm going to have to fix that before I go too. There's also the broken door on the hall closet that needs replacing and the window in the little kids' room that has to be unstuck. No way Anthony would ever get around to doing any of that.

This is going to be a longer list than I thought.

I'm rooting around in the top drawer for a pen when the phone rings. I recognize the number. It's Dad's office.

"Ahoy, matey," I say.

"Hello?" It's a voice I don't recognize.

"Oh, sorry."

"Would this be Patrick Armstrong?"

"Yes."

"This is Earl Colpitts. I work with your dad. You wouldn't know where he is, do you?"

"No. Why?"

"He didn't come in today for his shift and he didn't phone. It's not like him. We tried reaching him, but…"

The muscles in my neck jerk. Dad has never missed a day of work in his life.

"I've got a key to his place," I say. "I'll go see what's up."

The guy says, "Great. Thanks," and I promise to call as soon as I know what's happening. We're both making the effort to sound relaxed but we're both thinking the same thing.

This can't be good.

Chapter Ten

I get in the car and burn over to Dad's.
I buzz him from the lobby, but there's
no answer.

I didn't think there would be. I
keep hearing Earl say, "It's not like
him." That what scares me. Everyone
knows Dad would die rather than miss
work.

Dad would die.

I buzz again. The foyer hums with the sound of the fluorescent light.

No one's going to answer. I know that.

I punch in the entrance code, run up the three flights of stairs and open the door with my key.

"Dad?" I try to sound like I'm just dropping by. I try not to think of all those years he smoked and drank. I try to blank out that image of the legs on the floor in the Heart and Stroke commercial.

I walk down the hall.

The living room looks neat, bare, almost unlived in—but that's the way Dad always keeps it. The only signs of life are a pad of paper and a plate with a half-eaten sandwich left on the coffee table.

I say, "Dad?" again, take a breath and check the kitchen. He's not sprawled on the floor there either.

The dining room? Same as ever. Two chairs, a table, and on top of that, his ten-year-old laptop.

I switch on the light in the bedroom. The bed is made up all crisp and tidy. It looks like something you'd see in a motel. His bureau is polished. My graduation photo is framed and staring back at me from the nightstand.

Everything is "shipshape." Just like you'd expect from a guy who spent half his life in the Navy. Nothing is ever out of place.

That reassures me for a second— then it makes me feel worse than ever.

I swing around and look back into the living room.

That dirty plate on the coffee table.

Dad would never leave a dirty plate out. He'd wash it, dry it, put it away and wipe the counter before he sat down again.

My hands start to shake. I clench them into fists and tell myself to man up. Some soldier I'm going to make.

I look around. I notice the light on the computer.

Dad left his laptop on.

He'd never do that either.

My heart booms. I get this weird feeling like my body is totally hollow.

Something's really wrong.

Maybe I should call the police. I go back in the kitchen and grab the phone.

I start to dial 9-1-1, then think, What am I going say? My fifty-two-year-old father didn't show up for work three hours ago and he's not at home either?

Some emergency.

They're hardly going to put out a missing person's bulletin based on that. I'd be embarrassed even to ask.

Dad would be embarrassed.

What if he walked in right now from the gym and found out I'd sent the police after him? What if Earl just forgot this was Dad's day off?

Maybe Dad was taking a day off from doing the dishes too. It's not as if the guy doesn't deserve a break now and then.

I put the phone down, but my heart is still pounding.

The light on the computer blinks. I watch it for a while. Maybe Dad keeps a day timer on it or something.

I hesitate, then sort of creep up to the laptop as if it's a wild animal I don't want to piss off.

I reach out and hit a key. The computer groans and beeps, and the screen lights up.

Dad was looking at a website.

Paternitypro.com.

I forget about the day-timer idea.

I scan the site. It seems to be all about blood types.

This must have something to do with our little conversation at the Bluenose the other day. I don't know what the connection is exactly. Then I notice where the cursor is. It's under the line:

Two parents with A-type blood can't have a child with B blood.

I stare at the screen. I close my eyes, but the sentence is lit up in neon on the inside of my lids. I don't need to read any more. I know what this is about.

There's this pendant that guys in the military wear around their necks. It's called a dog tag. It's got their name on it and their rank and their blood type. I framed Dad's dog tag and a picture of him in uniform when he retired from the Navy. It's hanging on the wall right across from me.

I know what his dog tag says, but I get up and read it anyway.

John Patrick Armstrong
Chief Petty Officer, 1st Class
Blood Type A+.

Chapter Eleven

I don't let myself think too much yet. That would be a bad idea. I could just be making up problems where none exist.

I sit down. I take a moment. I figure out what to say and how to say it. I call Mom's office.

"Child Welfare International."

"Hi, Mom."

"Paddy! What's up?" She sounds so happy to hear from me. I get a stitch in my side and have to hit it with my fist before I can answer.

"I'm filling out a form for the Army," I say. "I've got your birthdate but I need your blood type."

"Oh. Well. That's easy. It's A."

I get that stitch again, only twice as bad this time. My eyes sting. I'm glad she can't see me.

"You're sure?" I say.

"I'm sure. I give blood once a month…Why would the Army need to know something like that?"

"Well…um…" There's so much crap on the Internet. How do you know what to believe? What if I'm wrong?

What if I'm right?

Her other line starts ringing while I'm trying to think of something to say. "Oh, honey, I've got to go. It's crazy here today. Let's talk when I get back.

I'm going to make that pasta you like with the tuna."

She hangs up. I stand there, still holding the phone. The way I'm looking at it, you'd swear it was a hand grenade with the pin already out.

I've got to get out of here. It suddenly doesn't feel right being in his apartment.

I'm walking out through the living room when I notice the pad of paper on the coffee table.

I should leave him a note. I'll just say—I don't know—I came by or something. We can talk later. Maybe I'll know what to say by then. I pick up the paper.

There's something written on it.

Dear Paddy,

That's as far as he got.

Chapter Twelve

It didn't matter what I was doing—playing hockey, playing in the band, studying for exams—Dad always had the same advice. "Keep your eye on the ball. Focus on what's important. Forget the rest."

It didn't come naturally to me, but I learned. I eventually got pretty good at blanking stuff out—but it's not working now. I keep hearing Martha say, "How could an old bulldog like you have a kid like this?"

Only difference now is she doesn't say it in that ha-ha, LOL-type way. She says it like, "Seriously. Think about it, John. How could an old bulldog like you have a kid like this?"

In my head, she actually wants an answer.

I don't want an answer. I want to forget about it. I want to get out of here but I can't even open the car door. It's like the keyhole keeps moving.

I try to concentrate but all I can think is: I'm not his son.

I'm not John Armstrong's son.

That means I'm not even Paddy Armstrong.

I get pins and needles all over my body.

What was my mother doing while he was away at sea?

My stomach cramps at the thought. I use both hands and finally get the key in the slot. I open the door. I get in the car. I tell myself to smarten up.

A couple of girls go by. I do my best to smile at them. They start to giggle. They look back at me a few times before they walk away.

Everything's okay. I put on my seat belt, turn on the ignition.

I remember this guy at the gym—some friend of Dad's—meeting me for the first time. He said, "Must have been some mix-up in the hospital, John. Looks like you took the wrong baby home."

They both laughed.

I sit up straighter, and the street sounds disappear.

Maybe that's all this was. A mistake at the hospital. Nobody had to be cheating on anyone else.

I pull out and head down Quinpool Road. Something comes back to me.

I saw an article in *People* magazine once about babies who were accidentally switched at birth. It happens.

Why couldn't it have happened to me?

Dad was on some ship in the Persian Gulf when I was born. (I have the postcard to prove it.) Maybe nobody was around to help Mom and…Maybe Mom was too tired and didn't really get a good look at the baby. It's not that crazy. She was exhausted after Olivia and Marlon were born.

Or maybe I'm just adopted and nobody told me yet.

I stop at a light and I start to get anxious again. I can't tell if it's my heart pounding or if it's just the guy in the next car with his bass up full-blast. The light turns green and we both pull out.

Who am I kidding? I'm not adopted. I know that. Mom's mother is always telling me I have the Newton eyes, or the Newton hair or the Newton sense of humor.

That means there couldn't have been a mix-up at the hospital either.

I'm Mom's kid. That much I know.

The car behind me honks, and I realize I'm holding up traffic. I turn left on Bayers Road.

Maybe the Navy made a mistake. Maybe Dad actually has B blood and he just doesn't know it. Big organizations like that are always screwing up.

No.

Dad gives blood too.

The guy knows his blood type.

Maybe...

My mind goes blank. I can't think of any more excuses. *Two parents with A-type blood can't have a kid with B blood.* There wasn't a mix-up. I wasn't adopted. Women can't get pregnant off toilet seats.

I see our house and realize that I don't know what *home* means.

I can't fool myself about this anymore. My father is fourteen years older than my mother. He was away at sea a lot. She was twenty and beautiful. She was probably lonely. Like, duh. What do I *think* happened?

I park in our driveway. I can't move. I feel like if I open the door and step out I'll be back in reality. I'll have to answer the question.

There's a moving van next door. A lady sees me and waves. She walks over. I can't think of any good reason not to talk to her.

"Hi!" she says. "I'm Sue MacLeod. I guess we're going to be neighbors."

I stand up. "Hi," I say. I try to look friendly.

"It's not hard to guess who you are! I just met your dad, and you're the spitting image. You've got the same nose. You must hear that all the time."

I feel the blood rush out of my face. There's the answer to my question.

"Yeah, I do," I say.

My voice must scare her. I leave her standing in the driveway with her hand over her mouth.

Chapter Thirteen

The little kids are sitting too close to the TV.

The only thing Anthony has to do all day is look after Olivia and Marlon, and he can't even do that right.

"Where's Daddy?" I say. That's what they call him so that's why I say it—but this time it almost makes me puke.

Olivia doesn't turn away from the screen. "Downstairs. But you're not supposed to bother him, Paddy. He's doing his yoga."

"Okay," I say and take them both by the shoulders and drag them back a few feet.

I head down to the basement. Anthony is sitting cross-legged on his purple mat, in a special yoga outfit that he ordered from California. The pants only come to his calves. They've got little slits behind the knees. If they were pink, they'd look like something Olivia would wear.

It's stupid but that makes me even madder. I try not to let it show.

"Hey," I say.

I know he hears me, but he doesn't respond.

I feel weirdly pumped. Not angry anymore. Just kind of alert. Like I'm standing in the wings, waiting to go onstage.

I lean against the washing machine and watch as Anthony pulls himself into another pose.

Pose. Even the word is embarrassing. What type of grown man poses?

He stretches his arms out straight to the side and puts one foot flat against the other knee. I'm sort of disgusted by the whole display. Then something about his hands gets me. There's this flash in my head and I know what it is.

They look just like mine.

He slowly lowers his arms and puts his foot back on the floor. He takes a deep breath, wipes the sweat off his face with one of Mom's good towels, then says, "Yes?"

"Didn't mean to bother you," I say.

"You didn't," he says. Clearly someone as lowly as me couldn't distract him even if I wanted to.

There's a glass on the counter. Anthony has to have distilled water and he can't drink out of plastic. That pisses me off too. He picks it up and takes a drink.

I say, "I just need to know your blood type for some forms I have to fill out."

Anyone else would realize what a lame question that is. Why would I need my stepfather's blood type for anything?

But Anthony is the center of the universe—or at least thinks he is. It sounds perfectly natural to him.

"Oddly enough," he says. "I do know my blood type. I sang on a cruise ship in the Mediterranean once. All the lead performers had to have a complete medical done. Insurance purposes, I guess. Lot of money invested in us..."

He yammers on and on. The guy never misses an opportunity to prove what an asshole he is. I let him dig himself in for a while, and then I say,

"Sorry, Anthony. What blood type did you say you were?"

He takes another sip of water. I never noticed before that we're the exact same height.

"B," he says. "B negative."

I knew he was going to say that, but it still takes the wind out of me.

I have this sudden urge to punch him in the face. One good punch and his nose would never look just like mine again.

I know I shouldn't hit him. It would upset the little kids if they heard noises and came running downstairs and found their father and me fighting.

I know I shouldn't do it, but I do.

Because Anthony's nose isn't the only thing I inherited. I have his temper too.

Chapter Fourteen

Anthony at least has the decency to say we were just pretending. That I was helping him prepare for a play. That I just slipped and we hit each other by mistake. That it's fake blood pouring out of my fist, fake glass all over the floor.

Marlon sort of falls for it but Olivia doesn't. She holds on to his leg, shaking, and looks at the blood running down my arm.

"I'm okay!" I say and muss up her hair. "It's make-believe." Like everything else about my life.

"I've got to get going now," I say. "Tell Mom I'll call her later."

I slip out the basement door and climb into the car out front.

I'm halfway down the street when I realize how bad I'm bleeding. I should have waited until Anthony put the glass down, but waiting wasn't really an option at the time.

I'm less worried about the cut than getting blood on the upholstery. Dad gave me the car. He said he didn't need it anymore. It's just an old beater, but he took really good care of it. He'd be disappointed if I messed it up.

I pull over to the side of the road. There's an old T-shirt under the passenger seat that I use to clean the windshield. I wrap it tight around my hand to stop the bleeding.

First aid. That's another thing Dad taught me.

Dad, I think.

I start driving again. I don't know where.

Can I even call him Dad anymore?

Do I call him John?

Call him, I think.

I pound my fist on the dashboard. I get a little jolt of pain, but I deserve it. What's the matter with me? Dad, John, whoever. I was supposed to be looking for him! The guy's missing.

How could I forget about him? He'd never forget about me.

I wiggle my cell phone out of my pocket and try to dial and drive.

The cut. The cell phone. Rush-hour traffic. It's all too much. I'm going to kill someone like this.

I pull into the right-hand lane and park with my ass half out in the road. Some guy lays on the horn. I'm too crazed to even give him the finger.

I speed-dial Dad. No answer.

I call Earl at the commissionaire's office again. He hasn't heard from him either.

I call my grandmother and my aunt Bev, but I don't want to upset them so I just make it sound like I have something funny I want to tell him.

I call the Bluenose. Martha hasn't seen him. She says, "Try the gym. He's been complaining that my rice pudding is starting to show."

I wait for a break in the traffic, pull a U-turn and head to Palooka's.

A girl named Sandi is on the desk. She's not supposed to give out information about clients, but I smile at her. I realize that's something Anthony would do. I don't care. It works. She checks the computer for me. "He hasn't been in for a couple of days—but people fall off their fitness regimes all the time."

John Armstrong wouldn't, I think, but I say, "Oh, okay. Thanks."

She notices the bruise on my cheek where Anthony actually managed to land a punch. "What happened to you?" she says. "Fighting over some girl or something?"

It's kind of funny, in a sick way, and I laugh. "Yeah, you could say that."

I ask her to call me if anyone knows where he is. She thinks I'm coming on to her but doesn't seem to mind. I put my hand up on the counter to write down my number.

"You should go to a doctor about that." She almost whispers it.

I look at my hand. Blood is seeping right through the old T-shirt. I'm surprised it doesn't hurt—then I realize that it does.

"Yeah, yeah. I'm on the way there right now," I say.

She hands me a towel to wrap it in. She's very pale. "All that blood," she says. "It can't be good."

I have to agree with her there.

Chapter Fifteen

I get in the car and lean back against the headrest. I look out at the parking lot. What a frigging mess.

My mother has basically lied to me my whole life.

My "real" father is an asshole.

The guys in the band have replaced me.

Tara dumped me.

Who does that leave me?

The Man Formerly Known as Dad.

I realize I've stopped using a name for him. I think of him and I see a picture in my head instead. A short solid guy with a close shave and a beige windbreaker. The guy no one else cares about except me and Martha. And Earl, I guess, at least when he doesn't show up for work. It's like he's an icon on my computer desktop now. Not a real person, just a symbol representing a function.

John Armstrong might not be my father but he's the only person I've ever been able to count on. Maybe I'm an idiot for thinking something's wrong, and maybe he really is just taking a couple of well-earned days off. But the truth is, I don't believe that.

My guess is he's sitting some- where, staring into space, looking at his life, too, and feeling just as bad as I am.

I'm going to find him.

I have no idea where to look but I'll figure it out.

I get out of the car. I peel the grimy T-shirt off my hand and throw it in the garbage can outside the gym. I wrap the clean white towel around it.

I remember him in his uniform showing me how to make a sling for a broken arm.

I think Navy.

I think ship.

Then I think boat.

His new boat.

He's on the *Julie-Anne*. I hate to think I inherited Anthony's intuitive side, but who cares? I know that's where he is.

And anyway, I've tried everywhere else I can think of.

I jump back in the car and slam the door.

Where did he say he moored the boat?

Herring Cove.

No, but it's close. The name of some fish.

Salmon? Mackerel? Tuna?

Halibut.

Halibut Cove. I get the map out of the glove compartment. Good old Chief Petty Officer Armstrong. I'd never have bothered getting a map for myself, but he made sure there was one here, neatly folded, when I needed it.

I spread it out with my good arm. Halibut Cove is about where I thought it was, only farther out. It'll probably take me an hour.

I check the time on the dash: 7:36 PM. No wonder I'm so hungry. I put the map back, only not as neatly, and find the energy bar he also left in the glove compartment for me.

I don't know if it's the "28 nutrients" in the bar that do it or the feeling that I'm on a mission, but I'm feeling okay.

It feels good to worry about someone else for a change.

Chapter Sixteen

I don't know what I'm going to say to him.

Maybe worse, I don't know what *he's* going to say to me.

I turn on the radio and just try not to think about it. But all the songs are about love, or making love, or cheating on someone. I turn the radio off.

I look at the scenery instead. The road runs along the ocean. At least that's pretty. I hope it will distract me.

There's a ship out on the horizon.

I can't tell from here if it's a Navy ship or a container ship, but it makes me think of Dad and what Mom did while he was away. I can't even look at the ocean anymore. I turn back and stare at the road.

To take my mind off things, I start to sing. I hum that little riff I was working on. Then remember what the song was going to be called.

B negative.

I snort in a way that could almost pass for a laugh.

I make myself think about Christie. She's a lot prettier than Tara. Better body. Nice smile. I try and hang on to that image of her and the thought that this time tomorrow night I'll be sitting across from her at the Nectar House.

But I can't.

Thinking about Christie, me and Tara makes me think of Anthony, Mom and Dad. And that makes me think of who I thought I was and who I really am and how I got to be that way.

Everything makes me think of that. I'm never going to be able to forget it. My whole life is poisoned.

I drive and drive and drive, and the same things just keep going round in my head. I suddenly understand how people go crazy.

By the time I get outside the city limits, I'm talking to myself. Fighting with myself. Telling myself to grow up. I'm just one step removed from those homeless guys who shuffle along the street, screaming at their invisible friends. I'm even starting to smell bad.

I pass a sign saying *Halibut Cove, Next Exit*. It snaps me out of it. I feel something sort of like relief. I don't know why. Maybe I just want to get it over with.

I turn off the highway. It's getting dark, and there aren't as many streetlights on this little road.

I drive for a while, and then the car starts to jerk and sputter.

I'm an idiot.

I slam the steering wheel with my good hand.

Gas.

I was supposed to get the light fixed on the fuel gauge weeks ago.

The car lurches. I manage to pull over to the side before it stops. The very first thing I think is, How many times did Dad tell me to keep my equipment in good repair?

I'm going to be embarrassed to tell him what happened.

I've always hated to disappoint him.

Then it dawns on me that he's got bigger things to be disappointed about than a busted fuel gauge.

Chapter Seventeen

I lock the car door and start walking. I try hitchhiking, but only two cars go past and neither stop. I can't blame them. I don't think I'd pick up a big guy with a bruised face and a bloody hand on a dark road either.

There are only a few houses along the way and they're pushed back from the highway. One has a light on, and I think of ringing the doorbell and asking for help, but I don't. Somehow I don't feel like I'm in such a hurry anymore.

The closer I get, the more scared I am. It's like I'm walking into a big black hole.

The road is really steep and I'm tired. My head throbs. My hand feels heavy. I make myself keep moving anyway.

I get to the top of a hill and look down.

That must be Halibut Cove stretched out below me. Even in the dark, I can see the white cabins of the fishing boats on the black water. One of them could be the *Julie-Anne*.

My heart starts up like a metronome.

The *Julie-Anne*. Some guy probably named it after his wife or his girlfriend. I wonder if that's why he sold it.

Would I still be sailing the *Tara-Marie*?

I get this sick picture of Anthony climbing aboard the *Maura-Louise* while Dad was away at sea.

I grind my eyes closed. Thinking stuff like that doesn't help. I shake my head, open my eyes and keep going until I get down to the water.

A dog barks somewhere off in the distance. Otherwise the place seems deserted. The little parking lot is empty and the asphalt's crumbling. Scraggly trees hang over the driveway. Doesn't look like Halibut Cove is used much anymore.

There's a rocky beach, which is slimy with seaweed, and an old wharf.

I climb to the end and almost fall through the rotten boards. I squint out at the water. Three boats are tied up in the bay. In this light I can't read any of the names. I can't even tell what color their hulls are now, but I notice a tiny red light on one of them.

It's a cigarette. Someone's sitting on the deck, smoking.

I cup my hands around my mouth. I call out, "Hello? Hello?"

I don't know if the person hears me or not, but there's no answer.

I've got to get closer.

For a second I think of swimming out, but that would be crazy. The water's calm, and it's not that far, but with this arm I'd never make it.

I climb down from the wharf and look around. There's only one street-light out on the road so it's hard to see. I fumble around the parking lot. There's an old metal shed, rusting away at the edge of the woods, but it's locked up tight. Someone seems to have dumped some garbage over to the side. I find part of a life-saving buoy under the wharf, but it would never hold me. I toss it back in.

It hits something. I lean in to look. There's a little upended aluminum dinghy. I don't know how long it's been there or how seaworthy it is, but it's better than nothing.

I pull it out and turn it over. There are even oars, though one of the blades is broken.

Good enough.

I drag the dinghy down to the water's edge. I slip on the seaweed and go under. My bad hand bangs against the oarlock. I can feel the pain right up to my teeth. I swear, get up, then slip again. I sit in the water up to my armpits for a good thirty seconds before I can make myself move.

Somehow I don't think this ever happened to John Armstrong.

I brace myself, steady the boat and get in. I start to row. My hand is practically useless. I have to keep giving a couple of extra strokes on the right side just to keep more or less in line.

My plan is to pull up alongside the fishing boat and ask the person if they know anything. I turn my head to see how much farther I have to go. I'm close enough to read the name.

Julie-Anne.

The man on board takes another puff on his cigarette.

"Dad?" I say.

"Nope. Sorry," he says. "I think you got the wrong man, son."

Chapter Eighteen

He doesn't even help me aboard. He's too drunk. I can see that immediately.

But he's also too drunk to stop me. I pull myself onto the boat and just try to ignore the pain slicing up through my arm. The boat tips from my weight, and bottles roll across the floor. He must have been here for a while.

He doesn't ask about the blood. He says, "So what are you doing here?"

I don't have a chance to answer. "Hope you're not here for your next child support payment, because I got some bad news for you, buddy." He flicks his cigarette into the water. "I closed that bank account."

"Dad," I say. It's just instinct.

He wags his finger at me. "Now that's got to stop. I'm Mr. Armstrong to you, boy." His voice is slurred.

He lights another cigarette. A little wave knocks the boat. A beer bottle hits my foot. I kick it out of the way. I'm suddenly mad at him.

Mad at him for drinking. Mad at him for taking off on me.

Mad at him for not being my father. Or at least not still acting like he is.

He takes a long slow puff on his cigarette, the way people do when they're wasted. It lights up his face for a second. I can see he didn't shave today. His hair is hanging over his eyes. I barely recognize the guy.

I realize what a prick I'm being. How can I be mad at *him*?

"Look," I say, "I know what you must be feeling."

"You do, do ya?" he says and laughs. "You know what it's like to be at sea, thinking you've got some sweet little wife waiting at home for you? You know what it's like to spend all your life and all your money looking after some kid who ain't even yours? You know what it's like to be taken for a fool?"

He raises his beer like he's toasting me. "Congratulations! Always knew you were a smart boy."

He downs it in one gulp, then belches. "I used to figure you took after my mother's side of the family. She was a schoolteacher, you know."

I nod. "Yeah. Granny Armstrong taught me the alphabet."

"*Missus* Armstrong," he says. "Granny's just for family."

He pulls another beer out of the box by his feet. Then he says, "Sorry! Where are my manners?" He tosses it to me and pulls another one out for himself.

"Manners. Maybe that was my problem! I've never been that cultivated a fella." He pops off the lid and tosses it into the water.

He winks at me. "I think maybe that's what your mother was looking for. Someone a little more, shall we say, refined. A little more educated. Maybe even a little taller. What do you think?"

I think he knows.

He stares at me and runs his tongue around the inside of his mouth.

"Well," I say, "I don't really…"

"Shut up!" He's never screamed at me before. "Speak when you're spoken to. I've had enough of you."

He sits there, staring at me. He's so drunk he's wobbling in his chair. He guzzles down his beer.

"Your mother and An-thon-y were in a play together once. Did you know that?" He's pretending to be polite. "I fortunately didn't get to see it. I was in the Persian Gulf, I believe, serving my country. I remember coming home and thinking how it kind of changed your mother. It worried me at the time. Thought I might lose her. But then I found out she was expecting a baby and I figured we'd be fine. Ha bloody ha, eh?"

He fumbles around for another beer. His eyelids are drooping so low I'm amazed he can see what he's doing. He manages to pull one out.

I could reach over and take it from him, and he'd be helpless to do anything about it.

I probably should. I know he doesn't need any more.

Or do I?

He's right. What do I know? What do I know about how he feels?

I change my mind.

I'm going to sit here with my mouth shut and let him drink and let him talk until he's said everything he wants to say. It's the least I can do for him.

Chapter Nineteen

It's pitch-dark out and it's really cold. I can't stop shivering. I don't know if it's because of my cut or hunger or if it's just because I'm so frigging tired, but I feel sick. I want to go to sleep, but he's still talking.

At least he's not so mad anymore. He just sounds sad now.

He's blaming himself. The drinking. Leaving Mom alone all the time. Not telling her how much he loved her.

He actually cries for a while.

Then he swears for a while just to show he's still a tough guy and opens another beer.

"I don't know how I never figured it out." He takes big long pauses between his words to take another puff or another gulp or just to keep his thoughts more or less straight. "Your mother's tall, so I assumed that's where you got it. She's a good-looking woman too. Too good-looking for the likes of me, that's for sure."

He has a big long laugh about that, then has to spit at the end of it.

"And I can't play a musical instrument of course. Not like An-thon-y."

He blows across the mouth of his beer bottle. It makes a humming sound. "The only song I know," he says. He laughs some more, but then his face goes serious again.

"People would say, 'Paddy's good with his hands, John, just like you.' Or 'Paddy's got your way with a tire wrench,' and I guess I just made myself believe that was proof enough. What a frigging fool I turned out to be, eh?"

He drops his head.

"You're not a fool," I say. "You raised me. You did what was right. You were a good father to me."

He doesn't say anything to that, but I think I got through to him. "I love you, Dad," I say. "I'll always love you. No matter what."

I reach out to put my hand on his shoulder and realize why he didn't answer.

He's passed out cold.

I go down below and get a blanket from his bunk. I put it over him and throw his cigarette in the water.

I push the bottles out of the way and lie down on the deck at his feet. I want to make sure he's all right.

Hopefully we'll both be feeling better tomorrow.

Chapter Twenty

I don't know where I am. I don't know
if I'm hot or cold. I don't know what's
happening.

Dad is holding my phone right in
front of my face.

"Paddy." He's not angry anymore.
"How does this work?"

I try to tell him but I can't figure
out how to get the words from my

brain to my mouth. My jaw bounces up and down like an old man's. Nothing comes out.

Dad takes my hand and puts it on the phone. "Turn it on, son. C'mon. You can do it."

This should be easy—I know it should—but I'm like a drunk trying to walk a straight line. I have to concentrate really hard to keep the world still. I lick my lips. I focus on the phone until there's only one of them. I see the button. I press it—but the screen stays dark.

Dad grabs the phone from me. "This button? This one?" I nod or at least I think I do. He hits the button again and again. Nothing happens. His face is gray.

I know what the problem is, although I don't know how I do. Did I dream it? I shake my head.

He says, "What? What's the matter?"

I'm afraid he'll be mad. He always takes good care of his equipment.

I want to explain that it was an accident, that I didn't mean to break it, that I just slipped on some seaweed, but all I manage to say is, "Wet."

Dad swears.

I see his feet walk back and forth on the deck beside me. I want to tell him I'm going to throw up but I don't have time. My insides spill out of me.

"That's okay," he says and wipes my face with the blanket. His face is really close to mine. He stinks of beer. His eyes are bloodshot.

"You're going to have to help me, son," he says. "We need to get you to a hospital. Can you get up?"

He pulls me to my feet. I see the veins in his neck bulge.

After that, I'm not really sure what happens.

Chapter Twenty-One

I sort of swim in and out of reality. It's like I keep falling asleep in the middle of a movie or something. I just have little video clips of what's going on, but they don't fit together very well.

The dinghy rocking. The sweat on Dad's face. Some guy stopping on the road. People running. Bright lights.

And then the tubes. I try to pull them out of my arm. The nurse puts her hand over mine and stops me.

I don't know if she tells me then or if it's something I overheard but I know I have blood poisoning from "the wound." That's what she keeps calling it.

Then sometime later—I don't know how long—I open my eyes and I see Mom. Her face is all puffy and wet. I suddenly understand how sick I am—but it's weird. I'm not scared. It's just sort of a fact.

I open my eyes another time and Dad's there. He's holding my hand and he doesn't let go of it even when he knows I'm awake. That doesn't seem strange either, although it clearly is.

Tara comes too. I've been dreaming about her, and when I wake up there she is, asleep beside me in the chair.

Maybe that's what finally knocks me back to life. I wake up for real this time.

I look around the room. It's sort of dark. The sun hasn't come up yet, or maybe it's just gone down, I don't know. There are flowers and balloons and cards everywhere. Dad is sitting bolt upright in a chair with his eyes closed and his mouth open.

I shift in the bed. I see someone's feet on the floor. I recognize them immediately. It's the tan. Anthony's asleep too.

Or maybe he's not. This game we used to play when he first moved in with Mom comes back to me. He'd be holding a bag of candies. He'd pretend to fall asleep and I'd sneak up to steal them. I'd just get my little hand on the bag—then he'd jump up screaming. He'd chase me all around the house until he caught me, but by then he'd be too "tired" to eat the candies himself. He'd end up giving them to me.

Anthony scratches his arm in his sleep, and another memory materializes in my head. I'm sitting on his lap. He's holding down the chords so I can strum the strings. It hits me that the person lying on the floor now is the same person who did that then. I hadn't made that connection before.

I touch Tara's arm and she jumps awake.

I say, "I'm thirsty." Her eyes smile as if I just told her I won the lottery. She runs out into the hall.

Dad and Anthony are both up in a second and crowding around the bed. They're smiling but they both look like they're not sure they're allowed to.

In a minute, Tara's back with the nurse.

"Which one of you is the father?" she says.

Dad and Anthony both say, "I am."

Chapter Twenty-Two

When I get out of the hospital, Mom tries to talk to me about it. She stands in the kitchen doorway, wringing her hands and blinking back tears.

"I didn't know," she says. "I mean, I didn't know for sure. It could have been either of them."

Just the way she holds her shoulders, I can see how ashamed she is.

"I didn't know what to do. I knew how much your father—I mean, John— needed me, and I knew how much he loved you."

Her words come out one at a time, as if they're ashamed too.

"So I tried to make it work. But John and I really weren't suited for each other...You can see that, Paddy, can't you? We split up for a while, and then Anthony came back to town and, well, that was that. I loved Anthony. I wanted to be with him. I wanted to have a husband who was here and talked to me and was interested in the same type of things I was."

I promised myself in the hospital I wasn't going to get mad. I was just going to listen. I was just going to try and understand.

"When did you know he was my father?"

"I didn't. Not really. As you got older

and taller, I started to wonder. But I just put it out of my mind."

Okay. I sort of understand doing that. "But how could you let him pay for me all those years? It doesn't seem fair."

"What else could I do? I couldn't turn down child support payments. John's a proud man. He'd never have let me do it unless I told him why—and that would have broken his heart."

She covers her face with her hands, but when she looks up she's almost pulled herself together.

"Maybe I was a coward. I don't know. But I was right about how much he loves you." She shakes her head. "I don't know how he managed to do it, but he got you off that boat and to the hospital all by himself. He stayed there every night and cried like a baby until you were better.

"He loves you," she says again. "And you know what else? Anthony does too.

I know you don't see eye to eye these days. But you forget. You did get along when you were little. He read to you. He goofed around with you. He taught you to play guitar. He tried his best. And you know he had a hard act to follow trying to compete with…"

She stops and figures out what to say.

"…with your dad. John's always going to be your dad, Paddy. And Anthony, I guess, will always be Anthony. That's just the way things are."

She reaches for my hand.

"I'm sorry this turned out the way it did. I really am. I'm sorry I put everybody through so much—but I don't regret it. I got you as a result and your dad did too. I hope you'll be able to look back some day and think you were lucky. You have two fathers who love you. They both gave you a lot and…"

She starts to cry. I don't know what she was going to say, but I don't need to.

I hug her. She sobs for a while, and then she realizes that I'm crying too and we both start to laugh.

"Oops, sorry. Am I interrupting something?"

Mom pulls away from me and wipes her face. "No, no, Tara. Come in! I was just going to get dinner started. We're having steak."

I put my arm around Tara. I don't even try to hide my tears. Neither of us is embarrassed by that kind of thing anymore.

A taxi pulls into the driveway. Mom looks out the window. "Oh, good, John's here. Paddy, will you call Anthony and the kids?"

I take a breath and I'm hit again by how weird this is, how hard this is going to be, how much we're all going to have to forgive or forget or maybe just ignore. For a second it almost paralyzes me.

Then I hear the doorbell ring and Olivia and Marlon screaming, "Papa John!" and the creak of Anthony getting off his yoga mat—and I'm okay again. Something tells me we'll be able to work it out.

We just have to be positive.

Vicki Grant left her career in advertising and television to write her first novel. *B Negative* is her sixth book, following *Comeback* and *Nine Doors*. Vicki's books have gone on to win many awards, including the prestigious Arthur Ellis Award. She lives in Halifax, Nova Scotia, with her family. More information is available at www.vickigrant.com.

Titles in the Series

orca soundings